Cock-a-doodle-doo, Creak, Pop-pop, Moo

by **Jim Aylesworth**

illustrated by **Brad Sneed**

Holiday House / New York

CH

Text copyright © 2012 by Jim Aylesworth
Illustrations copyright © 2012 by Brad Sneed
All Rights Reserved
HOLIDAY HOUSE is registered in the U.S. Patent and Trademark Office.
Printed and Bound in November 2012 at Kwong Fat Offset Printing Co., Ltd.,
Dongguan City, China.
The text typeface is TemaCantante.
The artwork was created with watercolors.
www.holidayhouse.com
3 5 7 9 10 8 6 4

Library of Congress Cataloging-in-Publication Data
Aylesworth, Jim.
Cock-a-doodle-doo, creak, pop-pop, moo / by Jim Aylesworth ; illustrated by Brad Sneed. — 1st ed.
p. cm.
Summary: Rhyming text divulges the many sounds heard on a farm, from a rooster's morning crow to an owl's goodnight call.
ISBN 978-0-8234-2356-9 (hardcover)
[1. Stories in rhyme. 2. Animal sounds—Fiction. 3. Domestic animals—Fiction. 4. Farm life—Fiction.] 1. Sneed, Brad, ill. 11. Title.
PZ8.3.A95Cnl 2012
[E]—dc22
2010041438

ISBN 978-0-8234-2754-3 (paperback)

To our beautiful Hickory Lawn Farm
—J. A.

For Grandma Johnson
—B. S.

Rooster crows,
Cock-a-doodle-doo.

Wake up, girls,

And little boys, too.

Old stairs *creak*.
Come fast as you can.

Ham *pop-pop*s
In the frying pan.

Cows all *moo*
In the milking shed.

Cluck, cluck, cluck.
Hens are being fed.

Sparrows sing,
Chirp, chip, chip, chip.

Mill wheel turns.
Drip, drip, drop, drip.

Tap, tap, tap.
Papa shoes the mare.

Peep, peep. Chicks
Running here and there.

Horses haul.
Clop, clip, clop, clop.

Chains *rattle.*
Kids riding on top.

Breezes *swish*
Through fields of wheat.

Clang, clang, clang.
It's time to eat.

Knives and forks . . .
Clatter, clink,
clink, clink.

Splash. The pump
Fills up the sink.

Yip, yip, yip.
Pups play in the yard.

Buzz, buzz, buzz.
Bees are working hard.

Cows *smack smack*,
All chewing their cud.

Pigs *grunt grunt*
In the nice cool mud.

Scrape, scrape, scritch
Scrapes the garden hoe.

Caw, caw, caw
Cries the coal black crow.

Whack. The boys
Are splitting wood.

Dink, dink, dink.
Cows come as they should.

Squeak, squeak, squeak
Rocks the rocking chair.

Crickets *chirp*
In the night somewhere.

Gramma knits
With *click clack clicks*.

Clock keeps time
With *tick tock tick*s.

Old stairs *creak*
Going up to beds.

Sniff, sniff, sniff.
Mice peek out heads.

Owl calls out
Hoo, hoo, hoo, hoo.

Good night,
boys,

And little girls,
too.

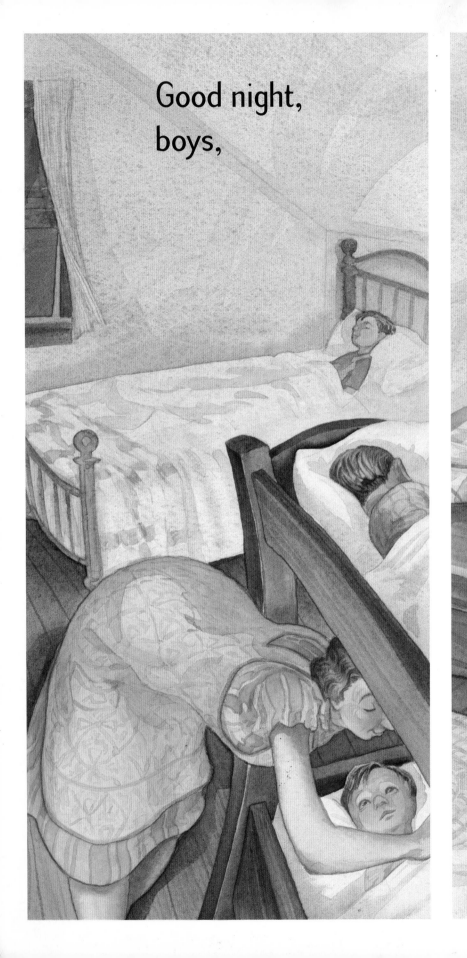